DUNCAN THE STORY DRAGON

DUNCAN THE STORY DRAGON

Amanda
Driscoll

Duncan the Dragon loved to read.

When Duncan read a
book, the story came
to life . . .

and his imagination caught fire.

Unfortunately, so did his book.

and his imagination caught fire.

Unfortunately, so did his book.

"I just want to finish a book," said Duncan.

"I need to know
what happens.

Do the pirates
find treasure?

Does the captain
save the ship?

Do aliens conquer
the earth?

"And I want to read those two wonderful
words, like the last sip of a chocolate
milk shake . . . 'The End.'"

Duncan tried everything to keep his cool.

Really.

Truly.

Everything.

"I have an idea!" said Duncan.
"I will find a friend to read to me."

Everything.

"I have an idea!" said Duncan.
"I will find a friend to read to me."

So Duncan
searched a nearby
neighborhood.

"Hello, friend," he
said to the raccoon.
"Would you please
read me this book?"

Duncan explored an evergreen forest.

"Hello, friend," he said to a possum. "Could you please read me this book?"

Duncan traveled to a faraway farm.

"Hello, friend," he said to the bull. "Will you please read me this book?"

After searching the entire countryside,
Duncan trudged back to his cottage.

As he hugged his book, a fat tear trickled down Duncan's cheek.

It landed with a plop . . .

dribble-drabbled across the floor . . .

then ran split-splat
into a mouse.

THE
FRIENDLY
DRAGON

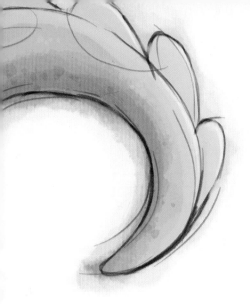

"Sad ending?" asked the mouse.
"I'll never know," said Duncan.
As Duncan explained his
problem, he noticed a twinkle
in the mouse's eye.

"Do *you* like books?"
Duncan asked.

"I LOVE books!"
said the mouse.

"Would you . . . could you . . .
will you please read me
this book?"

"Certainly!" said the mouse.
So the mouse read to Duncan (carefully).

Together they battled
sea monsters . . .

dodged icebergs . . .

. . . and discovered
new lands.

They took breaks for roasted hot dogs and toasted marshmallows.

Finally, the friends sailed home. Then the mouse read those two wonderful words, like the last sip of a chocolate milk shake . . .

But actually, it was only the beginning.

For Mom and Dad,

with two wonderful words . . .

"love" and "gratitude"

ISBN 978-0-545-94877-7

Copyright © 2015 by Amanda Driscoll. All rights reserved.
Published by Scholastic Inc., 557 Broadway, New York, NY 10012,
by arrangement with Alfred A. Knopf, an imprint of Random House Children's Books,
a division of Penguin Random House LLC. SCHOLASTIC and associated logos
are trademarks and/or registered trademarks of Scholastic Inc.

12 11 10 9 8 7 6 5 4 3 2 1   16 17 18 19 20 21

Printed in the U.S.A.   40

First Scholastic printing, January 2016

The illustrations in this book were created using pencil sketches painted in Adobe Photoshop.